Rose's Story:
Fifty and Fabulous!

Carla M. Cuffee

ISBN: 978-1-5356-1336-1

Preface

I wrote this book for myself, Carla C., using an alter ego. It's written in fantasy: "Can a girl live? Can I dream?" I wanted to write this book, as an alter ego, about how would I celebrate my 50th birthday.

Contents

The Introduction

Scarlet and Ruby Crystal are the daughters of Rose Crystal, who owns an event planning company named A Dozen Roses. She started her company back in 1986, picking up clients as far as California. Rose hosted small and large events, as low as ten and as high as five hundred. She could do lavish or purely basic. Everyone who was a part of the events was wowed. They enjoyed working with her because she was a pleasure to be around. She listened to her clients and gave suggestions as she saw their vision.

She was known just about everywhere she went. She was as beautiful as her name. In 2000, Rose met and dated a young man named Frank, who also had an upcoming growing business. Frank was known as "Big Eaze" to all his friends. Why the name Big Eaze, we really didn't know. The name of his company was called Big E's Enterprise. He dealt a lot in the music industry and food preparation. His company also set up banquet halls for Rose's events.

They dated for about ten years, and he mentioned many times in their years of dating that he thought it would be good if Rose thought about passing down her event-planning business to her daughters. Big Eaze thought he needed Rose; he wanted Rose to be by his side during his business affairs, meetings, luncheons, and travels. He also wanted Rose to be the face of Big E's Enterprise.

Rose gave it a great deal of thought and decided, "Why not?" Rose thought, *My jewels are all grown up now. They have helped me with countless events: engagements, weddings, sweet sixteens, bachelor/bachelorettes parties, company events, picnics, birthday parties.* She thought more and more about it. *Yeah, it's time to let my jewels shine.*

When Rose passed down the event business in the summer of 2014, the girls changed the name from "A Dozen Roses" to "Diamonds." The Dime Divas, as they came to be known, knew they had to go in it their way, to create a name for themselves. They did not want to live in the shadow of Rose.

The Dime Divas have now been in charge of the business for about a year. The company has continued to thrive. They host about five events a month. Now Rose was turning fifty, her birthday was approaching, and they wanted to give her a party. This is when the Dime Divas got to plan Rose's fiftieth birthday party, with all expenses paid.

Chapter 1

Meeting up

Ruby drove out to meet Scarlet. They wanted to meet up to go over the party details. They also wanted to meet up with Rose, so they agreed to meet at Rose's house.

When they arrived at Rose's house, Big Eaze (Frank) was in the front room reading the sports column.

"Hey, where's Rose?" Ruby frowned.

Looking up from his paper, Big Eaze said, "She might be in the kitchen with Bubbles. They were baking cookies for Bubbles' school bake sale."

"Awe okay. I didn't hear anything about her school having a bake sale," said Ruby.

Scarlet laughed. "Them little sneaks. It's probably for the both of them, and they just told you that, Big Eaze. They don't want to share with you! You don't know that line by now?"

They continued to laugh, while making their way to the kitchen to see Rose and Bubbles.

The mansion had about three kitchens. They found them in the smallest of the three kitchens.

"Hey, you two, what you're doing?" Ruby asked, even though they already knew what they were doing by the smell of baked cookies.

"We're here to start planning this party," said Scarlet. "And Rose, we know how you are and how you like things. We need some input from you," said Ruby while throwing shade Rose's way.

Rose gave them a glance. "We're baking over here and that alone is a lot of planning. We got sugar cookies, walnut chocolate chip, cake-like cookies, raisin oatmeal…we're baking about six different flavors. It's for Bubbles' school bake sale on Thursday." Rose looked at Bubbles to back her up.

"Yea right," said Ruby, "we're hip to that line. There's no real bake sale."

Bubbles was on her iPad, when she was supposed to be helping to bake cookies. Then she looked up. "Did I hear, right? Did I hear you say something about planning? Which always turns out to be work? Well, count me out."

They all looked at Bubbles and said simultaneously, "Bubbles, as if you're going to do any work."

"More like give orders!" said Ruby.

Again, they knew the cookies were not for some school bake sale.

At that moment, they all just sat around, laughed, talked, and had milk with some warm cookies. Even Big Eaze got in on some cookies.

Chapter 2

The Plan

For the next few weeks, Scarlet and Ruby continued to plan Rose's fiftieth birthday party. They planned for it to be a huge party.

They tossed around hosting the party at different venues. One that had sparked their interest was a castle.

Scarlet, with her eyebrow arched, looked at Ruby and mentioned, "What about a castle?"

Excited with that idea, Ruby said, "Yea, how super awesome would that be?"

So, it was. Rose would have her fiftieth birthday party in a castle. It was a girl's childhood dream, going to a ball, dressing in a puffy gown, running down a flight of stairs, and losing a glass slipper,.. ha ha ha (that's Cinderella story).

Later that week, Ruby called Scarlet to confirm that she had found or at least reserved a castle.

"It's on my, to-do list," said Scarlet. "In the meantime, we need to go over the color scheme, decorations, the food, music selections, the guest list, etc."

"This is not a surprise party. Rose should be involved; she is so picky," said Ruby.

"True, but we're planning her party, and we're the Dime Divas," said Scarlet, popping her head.

They both laughed, knowing their confidence in hosting their successor; they had it in them. They knew what was ahead, and they were not only up for the challenge but also for the party.

The list of friends that Rose and Big Eaze had, including their list of friends that Rose was also friends with, would surely mean the party would have well over a hundred people.

"Lights, camera, action please!" said Scarlet.

"You already know!" said Ruby.

Chapter 3

The Setting

Scarlet had a large network of friends with lots of connections. While out shopping, she ran into one of her friends who owned a couple of boutiques. She mentioned that she was interested in having a party at a castle.

Well, with just that conversation, a list of castles landed at her pedicured feet. She wanted to call Ruby with the good news. But with so much excitement, Scarlet pulled up the addresses for each castle via MapQuest and found one that was near an ocean. She called and scheduled a meeting.

Scarlet wanted to call Ruby right after meeting the attendant of one of the cutest castles that she felt would be the best fit for Rose's party.

Finally, Scarlet got the time to call Ruby to tell her that she had finally found the right castle. They met for dinner and she described the castle to Ruby. "It is breathtaking. The castle sits on a mountaintop that overlooks the blue ocean waters. A castle with high-peaked rooftops and stained-glass windows in every color of the rainbow. A castle that has a huge gold door that comes with a massive doorknob. A castle that's fit for our queen, Rose Crystal."

"Wow, that's pretty awesome!" said Ruby.

"Yup," said Scarlet, "and the party will start at dusk, 5:00 p.m. So, we should see a sunset that's out of this world!"

"I would love to drive up and see it one evening," said Ruby, "just to be sure of the timing. We want the right timing of when the sun will set."

"Right, and we want lots of pictures of a perfect setting: a castle sitting high above an ocean." Scarlet was really proud of herself. She kept smiling. Nothing could remove that contagious smile of hers.

"OMG!" said Scarlet.

"What! yelled Ruby.

"Did we or did we not add a photographer to our list?" asked Scarlet.

"Calm down." Ruby pretended to be writing "add a photographer to our ever-growing list." Ruby laughed.

"Real funny," said Scarlet. "Either way, little minor tweaks, I'm just so excited." She took a deep breath. "Things seem to be turning out great so far."

Scarlet checked an item off her to-do list.

Ruby already had her phone out. She kept a running tab of her plan of actions, her life journal, her goals, her to-do list, and her planner, but today was her to-do list day.

"We got the castle and the invitations." Ruby looked up at Scarlet. "Did we say finger foods or a full-course meal?"

"Well, it is a castle, so we should have a full-course meal," said Scarlet.

"And dessert," said Ruby.

"Yeah, like a birthday cake, (Roses birthday cake) a huge cake, possibly a four-tier cake with buttercream frosting," said Scarlet.

"Roses that comes in every color of the rainbow," said Ruby.

"Name written in gold," said Scarlet.

They laughed and blurted out suggestions before the other could get theirs out. They were so excited to be planning this big event. They wanted this event to be perfect. It was going to be such a huge crowd, and they were expecting to pick up more clients.

This has to be perfect, thought Ruby. *A window of opportunity lies at our feet, up for grabs, and we are grabbing it.*

Scarlet was just as excited to be bringing in her celebrity friends for Rose's party.

After the party, they were planning an all-inclusive seven-day Caribbean cruise vacation. And some of her girlfriends who had moved out of town were also invited to Rose's party.

We'll get together and have lunch/dinner, party of course, and then go over more details of this seven-day cruise, thought Scarlet.

But for now, it's all about Rose and her big fiftieth, thought Scarlet!

Chapter 4

The Castle

Scarlet had scheduled a meeting to view the floorplans of this majestic castle. Both girls were to arrive at the castle at 12:00 p.m. They had also scheduled a staff of forty from Big E's Enterprise to accompany the meeting. They wanted to arrive earlier than the staff for first views.

In their separate cars, Scarlet arrived before Ruby. The forecast called for a sunny day so Scarlet wanted to go in the castle and take in the views. She was wowed.

The sun peered in the stained-glass windows giving off a rainbow of colors. When coming back out, she met Ruby at the front door.

"Hey, diva," said Scarlet. "The castle is set up real nice; there's not much to do here. When Big Eaze moving team comes to set up the tables and chairs, this place will be a sea of elegance set in a romantic setting."

As they walked through the massive gold door, Scarlet thought it would be the right time to talk over the expenses with Ruby. It was only right, seeing as how the party expenses were coming out of Diamond's books.

While inspecting the castle, Scarlet turned to face Ruby and said, "Before the staff comes in, let's go over the expenses. I was shock that we both agreed on how much we were to spend on this event. Are we prepared if that budget were to expand?" (That was an easy way of saying go over the budget.) "I say all of that because I want to add ice sculptures of roses. It's not listed in our initial request, but I believe it goes well with the theme. The cost would be in the range of five thousand."

Ruby did a hard spin. "WHAT!" She was not at all upset with the idea of spending for Rose, but knowing how Scarlet loved to spend money she just wanted Scarlet to keep it at a minimum; bills still needed to be paid. "How many ice sculptures are we talking?"

"Well, we're here. We can see where they would be set up and go from there," said Scarlet.

"Numbers, Scarlet," said Ruby.

"Let's just say about ten. They are not very large ones," said Scarlet.

Well with that said, mention Ruby let that come out of your expenses, Ms. Scarlet Pooh! On second thought, we are looking to pull in more clients, and that's considered networking..."

"Which we are adding to our company revenue," said Scarlet.

While waiting for the crew to arrive, Ruby wanted to go over the floor plans once again. Scarlet became agitated. She had a small breakfast, and mentioned, "Let's call for some food and drinks. You know, from our favorite place… Talido's I'm in a mood for some Mexican food, while doing the cha-cha-cha!" (Her version of the cha-cha-cha)

"You do know that we can't bring in food if we don't order for everyone," said Ruby.

"Yea you're right," said Scarlet. "I'll just gnaw on this piece of wood." She pulled a granola bar from her Valentino bag.

In the meantime, Big Eaze crew of forty was just pulling up. The crew was in a luxury charter bus, one that Big Eaze traveled in when he had local meetings.

Sam, from Big E's Enterprise, came in first. The divas noticed her by her popping her gum. It was loud, more like a firecracker or small fireworks going off. *Pop, pop, pop, pop!* Very annoying. The castle was an empty vessel, so sound of any kind echoed.

Ruby had her hand held out in front of her. She stopped Sam in her tracks. "Wait just a minute. Not here with that smacking and cracking! I mean come on, that sound is offensive."

Sam rolled her eyes and kept on chewing her gum but chewing it much quieter. Sam shoved a list to the divas that had employees' names, job titles, their hourly wages, and their availability.

"Girl, stop with the attitude! You can be dismissed with no pay!" said Ruby while shaking her head. "How about those snap cracka pop snaps, Scarlet!"

After going over each person's position and what their responsibility would be for Rose's party, the hour was creeping past 5:00 p.m.

"Okay, time to wrap this up." mentions Scarlet & Ruby.

Everyone was advised on what day and time to arrive for Rose's big fiftieth (November 20 at 11:00 a.m.).

The divas said, "Please be on time. We'll be setting up the place promptly at 11:00 a.m."

Scarlet and Ruby thanked them all for their time and gave them a small black velvet bag of diamonds with their names written in glistening silver letters, which read:

"Diamonds"
The Dime Divas
Starring Scarlet & Ruby Crystal

Yes, they were fake diamonds. Heck, they gave them out to all their clients. It was a small token of appreciation. In that bag were about ten of the most beautiful fake diamonds. (lol) If you didn't know it, you would have believed that they were real. They served as their business cards. Its design was to wow the client, to bring them back with more business.

Smart idea, girls! Smart idea!

Chapter 5

In the Meantime

THEY ALL WANTED TO KNOW what each other was going to wear to the party.

Rose said, "Well, it appears that you lovely jewels are planning a beautiful party in a castle with stunning views of the ocean. We should dress up as we are going to a ball. And seeing as how it's my ball, I want to wear a champagne-colored gown that has a long train, dripping in sparkling diamonds. I want the light to hit my gown and give off a golden ray of light, like an angel descending from heaven. I want to be remembered as that precious jewel dancing the night away."

Bubbles chuckled. "Get your head out of the clouds, woman."

A rapture of laughter filled the room.

"Okay you'll see, and don't hate!" said Rose.

Scarlet wanted to show off her signature red lipstick.

How cool is it that she has her own signature line of lip ware, which she had been a part of way before being co-owner of Diamonds.

They all knew what she was going to wear, her all-time favorite color: white. It's the color Scarlet and her glam team wore when they were out promoting "**Scarlet Kisses**."

"Well," said Scarlet, "you already know that I stay in promote mode. So, my dress, I mean my gown, will be a form-fitted white gown, of course. I think I will also have a flowing train. No diamonds will need to be on it because"—with her index finger waving—"My shoes, oh my shoes will need to be geek out in diamonds," said Scarlet.

Rose, wide eyed, immediately stopped Scarlet. She was not happy that her jewel was trying to steal the spotlight. Well, at least that's what she thought.

"Huh? How's that?" said Rose. "Are you looking to get married? You're wearing white? (Trying to persuade her to change the color) Who are you, Cinderella?"

"Cinderella wore blue, Rose," said Scarlet.

Quickly Ruby got up, in her all sophistication, looking at each person, and standing proudly as she mentioned that she already had a gown.

"What?"

"When?"

"Where did you get it?"

Everyone was yelling at her at the same time.

Ruby laughed. "My gown is silky red and has diamonds on the neckline, the arms are in red silk chiffon with diamonds around the wrists, and, get this, it also has a train dripping in diamonds. It's a very sophisticated gown and it's perfect. It flows with my name Ruby. Hey, I had it made a while ago."

"What a minute, it is my birthday party. You can't outdo me." Rose smirked.

Rose was not a happy camper. She always loved to be the spotlight.

"Then jump out of a cake in that spectacular gown you're talking about!" Bubbles laughed.

"Enough with the jokes, Bubbles. Before I order a bubble machine just for you," said Rose. "What are you wearing, Ms. Bubbles, all of ten years old? You got any ideas?"

"Umm…" Bubbles thought about what she wanted to wear that incorporated her favorite color, purple. "I want to wear a purple puffy gown, a sweetheart jewel gown."

She was also an index finger waiver just like her aunt Scarlet.

"What is that, a boss chick moves or something? thought Ruby.

Bubbles continued. "I want my hair in curls and I wanna wear a diamond tiara, and yes I also want diamond slippers."

"Making sure we got all of her specifications in order. Well, here it is. We all seem to have picked the perfect gowns," said Rose. "Now for Big Eaze; this is going to be easy. Instead of him wearing a black tux, I think I want him to wear off white."

Big Eaze was walking in and heard the end of what Rose had said. Big Eaze went straight into a Michael Jackson spin and moonwalked! (lol)

"I'm going to be the best dress Dapper Dan there!" said Big Eaze.

They all cracked up because they all knew that Big Eaze loved to be flashy. His jewelry alone looked to be over a hundred thousand dollars: diamond rings, bracelets, diamond necklaces. He was a well-dressed man with the best rim hats a man could want.

Chapter 6

The Menu

Big Eaze had a list of employees, and a good chef was one of them. He hired the best in town. They had a kitchen of fifteen to host parties. They were set to meet with Head Chef Brew that afternoon. At that moment, Rose was the only one at the meeting. (The girls were running a bit late.)

Chef Brew sat quietly with his tablet out ready to take notes for the menu.

Rose, not wanting to keep Chef Brew any longer, cleared her throat and said, "I would like to have prime rib for beef lovers, stuffed chicken for poultry lovers, a vegetable medley, and maybe have rice. The one that we had at the last event. It had a lemony flavor? Or red potatoes."

Suddenly, Scarlet and Ruby hurried in. "Sorry we're late. We ran into major traffic," said Scarlet. Scarlet set her purse down. "We're the hostesses for this upcoming event, The Dime Divas, Scarlet and Ruby Crystal. Sorry to keep you waiting. So, I will go straight into the menu selection. I believe we agreed on stuffed salmon and seared red potatoes."

Chef Brew looked bewildered, looking at Rose and then Scarlet, not sure who was in charge of the menu.

"Huh? Have you already given him your menu selection, Rose?" asked Scarlet.

"Well, I know what I like," said Rose.

"Okay…" replied Scarlet and Ruby. "We're going with her selections. Can we at least be given the menu? We like to be aware of the selections."

"Yes," said Chef Brew. "I will forward an e-mail to Big E's Enterprise office inbox first thing in the morning." He got up, told the ladies have a good evening, and hurried out.

Scarlet watched Chef Brew in his quickness, scurrying out the door. "Not much of a talker," said Scarlet.

"The menu is done,"

"We have a castle, decorations, music, food, and not to forget a photographer. Oh yea, and ice sculptures." Mentions Ruby.

Rose's eyebrow raised. "Ice sculptures? I like that."

"Fifty only comes once," said Scarlet. "With that said, let's talk music selections. What types of music do you want played?"

Rose said that Big Eaze wanted to handle that area. "Big Eaze is currently in transformation when it comes to the music area. He is currently revamping his DJs and will be hiring a new crew. The first to be hired is…" Rose was in deep thought and could not think of his name. "Hmm…oh, DJ Spinn. He should be on board before my birthday ball. His resume is a long list of private parties; birthdays are the best days." She laughed. "School proms, weddings, car shows, fashion shows…I'm sure the list goes on."

"Okay we get it, as usual keeping it in the family," said Scarlet.

Great, thought Ruby, *a chance to have Big Eaze flip this bill.* So, she asked, "Will Big Eaze be flipping this bill?"

"Yup he sure will be," said Rose. "I'm meeting up with him and DJ Spinn for lunch. How about you jewels come have lunch and meet DJ Spinn?"

"No thanks," said Scarlet, "I have other plans"

They were getting ready to wrap up the meeting.

"I have to find a gift for someone who has just about all they want," said Scarlet. "It's going to take some time. If this meeting is adjourned…" said Scarlet. "I'll check you peeps later," she said while pulling her keys out of her Valentino handbag.

"Oh, I see you got your Range back," said Rose.

"YES…it took them long enough," said Scarlet.

"I miss my girl. After looking her over and all the detail my girl been under. She is pearly white, her leather shiny and clean, her music on beats, she smelling like a rich chick! She looks like she's smiling at me," said Scarlet.

Ruby could not believe what she was hearing but pretty much understood how Scarlet felt about her wheels. She felt the same of her black on black Maserati.

"Well, what about you, Ruby?" asked Rose

"Okay mentions Ruby where are we eating?"

"Merlet's," said Rose.

"Hmm…,"said Ruby.

"Hey, they got a mean steak," said Rose, "and you know how Big Eaze is when he has a new client. He goes all out on the meet & greet."

They all gathered their belongings while Scarlet was leaving.

Before she reached the door, Rose said, "Will we see you at dinner on Sunday?"

"Yup I'll bring the wine mention Scarlet

"Sounds good," said Rose.

Chapter 7

Lunch with Big Eaze

Big Eaze sat at the table alone but not for long. He looked up to see Rose and Ruby approaching the table.

"Hello," said Rose and Ruby.

"Hey, ladies," said Big Eaze. He was a bit surprised to see Ruby. "I didn't know that you were coming to this lunch meeting, Ruby. Where's Scarlet? It would be good for both you to meet DJ Spinn. I hear he's crazy good on those spin tables."

"She had other plans," said Rose.

"Okay," said Big Eaze, "but we will need to set up meetings where we are all able to meet in one place."

While pulling out Rose's chair, Big Eaze saw that DJ Spinn just had walked into the restaurant.

As DJ Spinn was walking up to meet with Big Eaze, he saw that there were others at the table. Spinn felt a bit nervous and thought, *this must be a three-in-one interview. I thought that this was a one-on-one business meeting with Big Eaze.*

DJ Spinn eyed Ruby at the table along with another lady. As he approached the table, he introduces himself. "Hello, I'm DJ Spinn."

"Yea, have seat, Spinn. No need to introduce yourself to me. But let me introduce you to these beautiful ladies," said Big Eaze.

Ruby already knew who Spinn was, but she waited to be introduced.

Big Eaze introduced Rose as his beautiful lovely Rose and business partner. He introduced Ruby as the entrepreneur, since she and Scarlet were given one part of the growing business in the event-planning business, one of the Dime Divas.

"Hello," said Ruby. "I'm pretty much familiar with your style of music. I've been invited to a lot of events that you spin at."

Spinn smiled. Okay, what you think?

Thinking to himself "I am trying to get hired here".

"You're good," Ruby said, smiling. "You pretty much have the crowd pumped up."

Oh, now Spinn was showing his pearly whites. Yea, spinning is my passion. Wherever I go, they let me get into my zone. So, it's only right to give it my all."

Big Eaze ears were wide open. He was impressed with this young man. He valued the Dime Divas' opinions.

It was a younger crowd that Scarlet and Ruby were handling right now.

With that, Big Eaze hired DJ Spinn. Big Eaze was concerned, regarding his current music transformation. He said, "Between the two companies that we run, there are a lot of events that go on. I'll depend on you to handle a pretty hectic schedule. You think you're up for that?"

"Yea, I'm up for challenge," said Spinn, looking at everyone at the table. "I love what I do; I love to spin."

"That's what I like to hear," said Big Eaze. "We need more DJs like you, young man, to keep the parties jumping! We'll schedule a meeting to go over some more details about the job; I'll have my secretary call you to set a time and day to meet."

"Thanks, sounds great," said DJ Spinn.

"Enough of this. Let's order some steaks." Big Eaze smiled.

Spinn stole another look at Ruby and smiled. He was really excited that she was at this meeting. *Sometimes it's hard trying to sell your style of DJing. I'll have to personally thank her later,* thought Spinn. *She's cute.*

They laughed and ate and Spinn talked a little about his spins across Seas. "I played in Europe and that was cool, but I miss home. I'm a homebody. My brother moved to Europe about four years ago. He manages this high-tech company. My parents and I visit him from time to time. It's pretty interesting there. But it's not for me."

Taking it all in, Ruby happened to look down at her watch. To her surprise, they had been at lunch for over two hours. She said, "Okay, good people, I have another meeting to be at within hour." She looked at DJ Spinn. "Nice to have met you. I'm sure we'll meet up to discuss things."

Ruby noticed that Spinn had gotten up to help her with her chair and coat. *Very nice,* thought Ruby

"Uhh…we will need to discuss the range of music. I'll have to get your number in couple of days," said Ruby.

"You'll have to also meet the other half of Diamonds," said Ruby.

"Okay sounds good," said Spinn. "It has been a pleasure having lunch with you as well."

Ruby, now facing Rose and Big Eaze, said, "You two have a good evening and I will see you at dinner on Sunday. I'll bring a dessert."

"Great," said Rose.

Chapter 8

SHOPPING SCARLET'S WAY

SCARLET CALLED ONE OF HER girlfriends to accompany her while birthday shopping for Rose. Not that she wasn't capable of shopping on her own; God knows that's not an issue. There have been times that when out shopping for someone other than herself, she fell prey to all the sales signs. Her famous line was, "I love to shop. I mean, there are so many good deals when I'm out here, and girl with my status has to stay on fleek!" A true diva. But today she had to focus.

Her girlfriend said, "Okay, so what do you think that Rose would like, or, better yet, what do you want to buy Rose?"

Scarlet said, "So I've been noticing," remembering Rose baking cookies, "that Rose has been baking lately. Maybe she would love a pizza oven. She does love a good pizza."

Her girlfriend's eyebrow arched. She said, "Really? When does Rose have the time to bake a pizza?"

Scarlet said, "Yeah you're right. What was I thinking?" She laughed at herself. "Uh, what about this idea. Remodel her home. I mean she has style but a good refreshing won't hurt a bit."

Her girlfriend looked a bit puzzled. "Wait, the entire mansion?"

Scarlet said, "No, wait, wait, wait. I got it. Rose does not have a home theater room or media room…Boom, there it is. Rose will be getting a home theatre for her birthday!" She cheered herself on, snapping her fingers and dancing. "Go me, go me, go me…"

Scarlet was truly amazed that Rose did not have everything.

"Hmm…how do you know that she wants a home theater?" asked her girlfriend.

"Look, that's something that she doesn't have, but she's getting it. And if she doesn't use it, someone will, best believe!" said Scarlet.

Chapter 9

Meeting DJ Spinn

Ruby needed to get DJ Spinn's phone number. *Time is closing in on us, and we need to go over the music selection. It's time to schedule a meeting with DJ Spinn. He also needs to meet Scarlet,* thought Ruby.

Ruby called Big E's Enterprise and with one ring Sam answered. "Big E's Enterprise, how may I help you?"

"Hi, Sam, this is Ruby."

"Hi, Ruby, what can I help you with?"

Wow, her attitude has changed, thought Ruby. "I need DJ Spinn's phone number. I'm sure we should have it on file by now."

"Okay let me check. Please hold the line," said Sam. Within minutes, she came back on the line with DJ Spinn's number. "Hi, Ruby, I have DJ Spinn's telephone number. It's…" and she recited the number.

"Thanks," said Ruby, "have a good day." But before hanging up the phone, Ruby listened for Sam's response.

Sam said, "You have the same," and she hung up.

Ruby was taken aback. *Wow, she is really pleasant today. I wonder what's come over her? I'll have to find out later.* still remembering the last time, they saw Sam she appeared to be in funky mood.

Ruby called Scarlet and told her that she had DJ Spinn's number and wanted to schedule a meeting that week.

"What does your schedule look like this week?" asked Ruby.

"Do you remember that dance company that wanted to host an event? Well, I saw one of the co-owners who wants to schedule a meeting this week," said Scarlet.

"Did they give you a time or day?" asked Ruby.

"Not to lose them as a client, I gave them Wednesday at 12:00 p.m. Would that work for you?"

"Yeah, Rose's birthday party is a pretty big event. We'll get more information from them and juggle between events."

This was nothing new to the divas. But they would love to come together just one time and agree on upcoming events.

Their lifestyle had grown a bit hectic this past year. They have mention in near future in hiring personal assistants, which is very much needed.

"Okay, what I'll do is call DJ Spinn and find out what day and time would best fit his schedule. I'll call you back," said Ruby.

Ruby made the call. Voicemail came on and directed the caller to leave a message. Ruby left her information and went about her day, while checking the Internet for gift ideas, which was still on her to-do list. She thought, *I wonder what Scarlet came up with*. Ruby checked her watch. Over an hour had passed and no call. She continued checking the Internet, and then her phone rang.

DJ Spinn was on the other line. "Hey this is Ruby. Scarlet and I would like to schedule a meeting with you. What's your schedule this week?"

Spinn already knew his schedule for the week. Big Eaze was not kidding; he held a very busy schedule. "This week I have an event every day, but we could meet at a specific time and place," said Spinn.

"Good. What time is best for you? I have an upcoming appointment on Wednesday at 12, so that day is out," said Ruby.

"Oh okay, how about Friday at 4:00 p.m.? My next spin is not until 11:00 p.m. that evening at The Glow."

Not to mix pleasure with business, Ruby stayed focused. She knew exactly where The Glow was. "Okay, that sounds great; 4:00 p.m. it is." She continued to give Spinn the address on where to meet. "How about we all meet at Vested the restaurant on 9th?"

"Okay that sounds good," said Spinn.

"Great," said Ruby. "And by the way, Scarlet and I are hosting that event at The Glow."

Spinn seemed to be excited. He figured that he and Ruby would meet up and get to know each other more. "Yeah, well, I guess we'll see each other there. Do you dance? I mean, I made this new track this week, which gives me about one hour of free spinning."

"Of course, I dance," said Ruby, "but I'll be working. So, for now we'll see you on Friday at 4:00 p.m. okay? Have a good week." She then hung up her phone.

Spinn looked at his phone. *Woo, she's cold.* He hung up his phone.

Chapter 10

Selected Music

Ruby set up to meet at the hottest newest restaurant in town, Vested, owned by one of her childhood friends. She reminded DJ Spinn via voicemail and texted Scarlet the address on what time they were to meet. Both had been on separate schedules this week.

When Scarlet and DJ Spinn finally arrived at the restaurant, Scarlet was impressed with the place. She arrived earlier than Spinn. She walked in and spoke to the pretty young lady behind a tall glass desk. "Good evening. I have a four o'clock meeting scheduled under Diamonds."

"Your name please?" asked the hostess.

"Scarlet Crystal."

"Yes," said the hostess. "There is one already here under Diamonds. Please follow me." She picked up a menu.

As she escorted Scarlet to her table, Scarlet checked the hot spot out, thinking, *umm…I need to schedule our girl's vacation dinner here, and whatever they're cooking right now, smells delicious!*

Vested was a well-loved restaurant with lots of lighting—some bright, some dim, some even gave off rays of colors near the bar area. The furniture was wrapped in lots of vibrant colors, giving off good vibes. The pictures adorning the walls were of famous settings across the world. The sitting areas looked very plush and comfortable. Scarlet laughed to herself. Without a doubt, she would be setting up a dinner party soon!

The hostess escorted Scarlet toward the lounge area where they were to meet up with Ruby. The Hostess gave them her name (my name is Carla) and handed Scarlet the evening menu while mentioning, "You ladies have a great evening."

"Hey, diva," said Scarlet, "this place is hot. I love the vibe here. Who owns this?"

"Awe, I think you know him. Lloyd. Yea, he's talked about owning a restaurant when we were kids," said Ruby.

"The food is really good here, and the prices are pretty reasonable."

"I'm proud of him," said Ruby with a small chuckle. "Owning a restaurant is a lot of work. I have to hand to him; he's doing a great job. Vested has been up now for about eight months and doing well."

"Well okay," said Scarlet, looking over the menu. She knew exactly what she wanted. She thought every restaurant should carry a salmon salad. "You sound like a commercial. Are you part owner or something?"

While waiting on DJ Spinn to arrive, the divas talked about the meeting they had on Wednesday.

"I think the meeting went as expected," said Ruby. "We'll have to clear a week in our schedules to get somethings together."

"It doesn't seem to be on huge scale. But you never know; it is open to the public so we need to plan like it's a huge event. We'll go over the figures later," mentions Ruby, which Scarlett agreed

Scarlet knew how hard it was for the both of them to clear a full week, but they'd work on it.

At that moment, Spinn was walking up to meet the divas. "Hello," said Spinn.

Ruby introduced DJ Spinn to Scarlet. They shook hands.

"Nice to meet you," said Spinn.

"Likewise," said Scarlet. She also had been at his Spinn's parties. "I here you'll be at the Glow tonight." ask Scarlet

Yup. Getting my groove on," Spinn said, now looking at Ruby.

Ruby sat up straight and cleared her throat. She thought, *not trying to date at work.* "Excuse me." Ruby looked over the menu. *Umm…but she already knows what she's ordering.* She wanted to break up the stare from Spinn.

(as if we're going to meet there, like a date oops No).

The waiter arrives and asked if they were ready to order. Each one ordered: one steak salad, a salmon salad, and Spinn ordered a 100 percent blue cheese Angus burger.

"Well," said the divas, each speaking after each other. Spinn's eyes moved back and forth to each diva. He felt like he was spinning.

"Why we're here…to discuss the music to be played at Rose's fiftieth birthday party. We like to have the 70s up to current music played, you know, mix it up," Ruby said. "Keep the crowd pumped up, let them feel as if they are the DJs."

"Yea, like they own the music. You know, when the music is so good, people walk to a different beat," said Scarlet. "That's how we want this party to go." She had an index finger in the air.

"Spin as if this is your last spin!" laughed the divas.

Woo, I see these divas are serious about their events, thought Spinn. "Hey, ladies, I'm the man for the job. I know you heard; you'll see tonight."

"We've been at your spins, but we want more." Scarlet gently pounded her hand on the table, not to attract any attention. "No disrespect, you're good. But we expect great," said Scarlet.

"Great music and great food brings more clients," said Ruby.

Spinn gave them a list of music that he had in his possession and said, "If there is anything else you ladies would like to hear, let me know right away. If I do not have it, but I doubt it, I will make sure that I get it."

They scanned the massive music lists, highlighting music that they thought Rose would enjoy.

Spinn checks out their selections and thought, *I'm not going to be held to a list of music. I'm doing my own thing. They'll see and I'm sure that they will love it. But I'll go along for now.*

It was approaching 6:00 p.m. so they wrapped up the meeting.

Spinn stood first. "Either I will or will not see you ladies this evening. If not, then have a great evening."

"Yes, you too," said the divas. They too got ready to leave.

"We may not see you, but we will hear you at The Glow, so enjoy the night," said Scarlet.

Spinn did not look back. He just walked out thinking, *these divas are fierce!*

Chapter 11

Time

Ooooooh it was time to parrrrrrtayyyy!

Rose fiftieth birthday was in two days, and everyone who was participating was very excited! The dresses had arrived and they were beautiful.

They all gathered at Rose's house. They walked into her massive walk-in closet. It was so bright, and the light hit the marble floor, giving off rays of brilliant colors.

Under this glow I mention, I have arrived! chuckle Ruby

The room was far from being a walk-in closet; it was more being like a small boutique! Rose's countertops were cast in tinted sky-blue glass like the sky, and there were mirrors everywhere. It was sure to capture a glimpse of every part of you. The size of this room was amazing! Everything was beautiful: the cream-colored wall-to-wall cabinets, glass doors, and crystal chandelier that gave off a rainbow of colors. One can imagine being in this fairy tale, getting dressed for the ball.

Rose had great taste in colors. Creams, pinks, black, blues, greens, crystal, and tinted glass could be seen throughout the room. Her shoe rack, rather, shoe wall had well over a thousand pair of shoes from flats to wedges to heels, and boots in all colors, having its own lighting fixture. She had a ladder that was rimmed in diamonds just to get to the tallest of shoes. The room gave off a pleasant smell of Tender by Burberry Body, wow! With the amount of people in there, the room temperature was pleasant and not at all stuffy.

Everyone was chattering and laughing and having a great time. There was ample space to try on gowns.

Rose standing off in a corner I see that Evelyn had brought up tea and cookies. There's never a dull time in this place. In this very moment, this is one of my favorite place to be sitting. Believe me it feels peaceful, I feel welcome, happy, a place where I can dream, and dreams do come true! I can sit in here all day, either daydreaming or reading a good book or writing a good book. It definitely doesn't feel like your basic closet.

I was brought up to have class, style, charisma, and a mind of my own. I know how to make a girl feel like a princess! Well, enough of this standing around. Time to try on my gown

Chapter 12

The Big Day

Rose was up early. She was up before anyone could say happy birthday. (That's what she thought.) As Rose approached the kitchen, the aroma of fresh brewed coffee enlightened her taste buds. Rose stood near the huge brown marble island in deep thought. *I need coffee, and I need my quiet time.* She appeared to be a bit nervous. *Everyone's home and when they awake, it's sure to be a loud and busy day.*

Evelyn walked into the kitchen, and Rose thanked her for making the coffee. Rose asked her to wait about an hour before making breakfast. She said, "The smell may wake them and you know I need my 'me' time," while patting Evelyn on her arm.

"I understand," said Evelyn in a heavy Spanish accent voice. "I see everyone's home and it's your big day. Happy birthday."

"Thank you," said Rose, smiling with excitement but trying to stay cool.

Rose poured her a cup of coffee in one of her favorite mugs—a pink twenty-ounce mug rimmed in crystals. She took her coffee, walked to her favorite room, and sat in her favorite bay window, which overlooked a massive garden filled with flowers in every color a mind could imagine. The garden also housed a rock garden and a large gazebo near a small pond. She now seemed to be in a peaceful mood, sipping her gourmet coffee.

She meditated, reflecting on her fifty years of life, and gave thanks for good health, her family, and her fortune. As she looked out the bay window, she timed the sunrise.

She was wowed with all the colors in the sky—the deep pinks, the lavenders, the backdraft of the dreamy blue sky. It was a sight to see and she was very thankful that she had the opportunity every morning to see God's beautiful canvas; it set the mood for her.

She was not even halfway through her coffee when she heard footsteps. The door creaked open. In a whisper, she heard a familiar voice call her name.

She sighed. "Well, that's done. My view and my alone time are cut short." Rose answered, "Yes," trying not to be loud.

Rose didn't have a clue, but her family and her staff had gathered in her favorite room ready to sing "Happy

Birthday." They had it planned all along. They were very aware that Rose liked it very quiet in the mornings. They were going to surprise her in a low version of the "Happy Birthday" song.

All in one big whisper, they sang, "Happy birthday."

Rose was floored. They sang in such a beautiful tone, as if it was practiced many times until it was perfect. Rose was touched and thanked them all for that beautiful gift of song.

After the birthday song, she welcomed all who wanted to take in that beautiful view of the sunrise, which now was a glowing ray of sun.

While breakfast was being made, chatter and laughter filled the room. The one big thing everyone talked about was this evening at the birthday ball in a castle. All were smiling and ready for the night to begin.

"It's going to be magical night to remember," said Scarlet and Ruby.

Chapter 13

Busy, Busy, Busy

Scarlet and Ruby drove separate cars to meet at the castle at the designated time (11:00 a.m.), ready for Big Eaze crew to arrive. As they got out of their cars, they saw a charter bus coming up the hill...

"Okay," said Ruby, "here comes, the crew. The party truck should also be arriving." Just as Ruby mentioned it, they saw a big truck at the bottom of the mountain hauling up the hill.

They both looked at each other, as if to say, "You ready?"

The crew got off the bus one by one, all dressed in black and white uniforms. Sam also gets off the bus. She was dressed in a form-fitted black dress and held a black portfolio.

Scarlet and Ruby walked over to greet them, and in one voice said, "Good morning, ladies and gents."

Scarlet continued, "Today is going to be a busy day for you. But I want you to also enjoy this day. You also are attending this party, so I expect some level of professionalism."

By now, the truck was approaching the top of the hill along with other cars.

This is where we need more help, thought the divas. Keeping it in a control manner, Ruby stepped off to greet the driver.

The driver parked the big rig, got out, and introduced himself. "Hi, I'm Joe. We're from Big E's Enterprise and we're here to unload items for a party." He then walked to the back of the big rig and opened the massive doors.

Ruby noticed that DJ Spinn had parked and was approaching her.

"Hey you mention Ruby." Both were smiling. "Busy, busy, busy!"

The truck was filled with tables, chairs, lighting equipment, large palm plants, small and large boxes labeled "decorations," everything one needed to host a large party.

Head Chef Brew also approached the crew and said, "Where I can be of some assistance?"

Scarlet, now standing in front of a well-groomed castle, said, "Thank you all for coming out on time. Let's get this party started." She turned around headed to the castle's massive gold doors. She then turned back and said, "CHARGE! No, I'm kidding." She giggled. "Follow me please."

Big E's Enterprise crew started unloading the truck with tables first. Everyone worked hard. The lighting crew worked hand in hand with the music crew. They set up strobe lights and lights that shimmered in a soft, white glow, almost having a golden effect.

DJ Spinn was in practice mode, playing music that everyone could relate to. His crew set up the dance area, now all decked out in shimmering/strobe lights.

The flower crew, not to interfere with the table crew setting up their tableware, placed a bouquet of colorful roses in fancy vases on all the tabletops. They smelled and looked so beautiful!

Not to forget the food preparation on deck chopping and slicing and grinding. It was music to their ears. The shaved ice sculptures were in the processes of being carved into bouquets of roses.

The alarm went off and the divas looked up; it was now close to two o'clock. They took a step back. They were in awe! The tabletops were set in a romantic setting— ivory colored rimmed in gold covered chairs with matching tablecloths. Champagne glasses were on every table with glowing candles flickering in the Hawaiian breeze. Roses mixed with baby's breath were in colors of a rainbow. Soft music came from the large speakers, which set the mood of romance. The ice sculptures were now completed.

They had their own lighting to show off a mixture of colored roses.

"Oh, my goodness! Said Scarlet This is so beautiful, so romantic. Yeah Ruby agreeing this is so on another level!

Chapter 14

Heading Out

Big E's Enterprise crew was way past gone. They had finished about an hour ago. They packed up their belongings and the crew got in their cars heading down the mountain.

Ruby noticed Joe and Sam talking. Sam was smiling while Joe got in that big truck, backed up like a professional, and headed back down the mountain. Sam turned to come back to the castle and noticed that she was being watched. She said nothing as she walked by with a smile on her face. *Hum! We see a romance brewing.*

The crew of forty had just finished their sections and were all standing around talking and taking in the views of the blue ocean waters.

Both divas overheard a staff member say, "I have never worked in a castle, let alone on top of a mountain overlooking an ocean…Wow! Rose deserves this. She's such a beautiful, kind woman. I would love to do something like this for my mom."

Ruby and Scarlet were touched by that comment. They knew it was a privilege to do this, to live this lifestyle. They never took anything for granted and always gave thanks.

As they approached the crew, knowing they were heading out to get dressed for this special occasion, they thanked them all and advised them to take their hour and a half break. The staff was welcome to take in the sights. Their bus was there to take them down the mountain into town. They asked everyone to be back no later than 4:00 p.m., ready to greet the first guest with a smile!

Chapter 15

Countdown

While arriving at Rose house, the music was blaring. Everyone, including the staff, was in the halls dancing. The divas were very puzzled. "What, what's going on here?" asked Ruby, to all who seemed to be in this dance frenzy. "You *do* know what time it is, right? We only have three hours to get dressed, for starters, hair, nails, and makeup needs to be done!"

No one was listening to her; they were grooving, worrying more about getting their dance on! To their amazement, the divas just looked at each other and started dancing!

(see you got to live in the moment)

They were having such a good time. why stop them now!

Rose & and Big Eaze did their two-step. Scarlet was in her groove, looked over her shoulder, and told Rose, "Hope you got more than that. You're going to need it, missy. You're not going to just sit around and mingle with the guests; you got to dance tonight."

Now everyone started a Soul Train line, each one doing his or her very best to out dance the other with their dance moves:

The Robot

The Snake

The Running Man

The Electric Slide

The Harlem Shake

Of course, Bubbles did the Shmurda

Evelyn did The Wobble (big girl back it up)

Oh no they didn't…The Cabbage Patch

The Dab

Yea, of course, The Two-Step (if you don't know anything else, you got that)

This went on for at least fifteen minutes. Someone had to stop this. How would it look for the birthday girl to be late to her own party?

"Okay, okay, okay STOP!" said Ruby, hands waving frantically.

Everyone just froze in their dance position, shucked the dust off their shoulders—like they were in a Jay Z video—and went on their merry ways, as if it never happened.

The divas thought it was straight crazy, but they loved it.

Chapter 16

All Dress

Hair, nails, and our makeup were finally done (now that was cutting it close) thought Scarlet.

We all met on the spiral staircase, like a prom lineup.

I have to admit, we were stunning, our gowns glowed like lights on a Christmas tree.

As we all stood there modeling for the staff at the bottom of the staircase, who marveled and applauded. It wasn't hard to feel like we were awarded a prize, a prize of approval and honor.

We relished in that moment, taking it all in.

We had about two hours. Pictures were taken, in groups, some done separately.

I'm still stunned on how we pulled off the timing. With everyone in a dancing frenzy, some would think that they surely would not make up the time.

But we have a host of assistants, and they are paid a handsome salary to work their magic.

See when we host events, we have hairstylists, makeup artists, and a wardrobe staff, down to the shoelaces; and they would help put on pantyhose if needed. It was important for us to look & and feel our best, it's our job & we take pride in it & we take pride in our huge staff they make us look our very best, it's a brand & their apart of that brand, which they take pride in their jobs & with that everyone's happy!

Before leaving out, Rose addressed everyone. "I'd like to thank my beautiful daughters (my jewels) for making this happen. I have to admit, in my entire career of hosting events, I have never hosted an event in a castle, let alone overlooking an ocean. I'm very impressed with them thinking outside the box, and I wish them much success. Never stop believing in your dreams; reach for them and make them come true. If one doesn't go right, go back to the drawing board and start over. Never give up and never give in. To the staff, thank you for your patience, and thank you for hanging in there. You're an awesome crew and I appreciate you all! With that said, let's go to the ball!"

The limousine was waiting outside with doors open, and the staff that wanted to take the charter bus gathered on one of Big Eaze luxury charter buses.

We had minutes to get to the castle, which we were scheduled to take more pictures.

Chapter 17

On the Move

ALL THAT COULD BE HEARD were sounds of laughter in that stretch limousine, which by the way was a Range Rover decked out in pearly white with diamond accent rims; even the wheels were as shiny as a sunray. The inside seating was laced in white leather, and all the headrests were incased in diamond-accent embroidery. There were so many diamond effects going on in this limo, they felt like a diamond tycoon. Even the outside mirrors had the same diamond effect.

The ride to the castle was about a twenty-minute ride, so there were filled champagne glasses passed around, except for Bubbles who would get 7-Up.

Each face was filled with joy. They were so excited about this day that had finally arrived. The divas figured that since you only turn fifty once, so live as if you're turning fifty over and over again.

The aroma of perfumes and beautiful new gowns and tuxedos, along with leather and clean car freshener and the sipping of champagne…gave them the appearance of wealth. It would have seemed that it was the very first time they had ridden like this, but Rose had done it countless times. She had been invited to affairs of the most important people of the country; kings, queens, prime ministers, ambassadors, and high government and state officials had invited her to their functions. But this day was so special to her. She had turned fifty. She had reached a milestone in her life and it was a very special day, a day of riding along with her daughters and granddaughter (her precious jewels) and Big Eaze, her significant other.

The limo finally stopped the door opened. There were droves of cars in the parking area. Rose stepped out of the limo and everyone was in awe. She greeted them with a princess wave.

The greeters greeted each guest at the front entrance of the castle. They were assisted to their seating areas and served some refreshments while they waited and mingle with other guests until the ball was to begin.

Rose and her family took pictures before they went into the castle, which took about forty-five minutes. The views were breathtaking. The castle sat alongside a mountaintop overlooking the blue ocean waters under a backdrop of the most gorgeous of sunsets. God must have been impressed because the sunset was such a dreamy one (red with orange rays). From where they were, they had the best view of the sunset.

When they were done taking pictures, they entered the great ballroom. The divas were to go in first, even though the guests had already seen Rose. She and Big Eaze were to make a grand entrance nestled arm in arm, with Rose dressed in that perfect designer gown made just for her. The train, which spoke of elegance and richness, flowed like water flowing down a riverbank.

Chapter 18

The Entrance

Rose was to make her entrance. The announcer, in a high-pitched, squeaky voice, bellowed, "The queen, the queen, the queen has arrived!" Everyone stood to greet the queen.

A glow of lights and a small, misty fog started, and with fist pumping, DJ Spinn had the music pumping loud. Rose strutted in on "It's Going Down for Real" by GDFR (the clean version). She wouldn't have it any other way.

She blew kisses at the crowd as she passed by, and the crowd went into a frenzy. She really pumped the crowd when she dropped it, popped it, shook it. When she threw her Emirates in the sky, the crowd roared like it was a concert. It was quite an entrance!

In shock, Big Eaze took a step back, arched his eyebrows, waved his arm in the air, and said, "It's going down for real!"

Now that was an awesome entrance! They did their thang!

"Lift it, drop it, shake it, pop it! ...It's going down for real!"

Chapter 19

She Mingles

Rose and Big Eaze were guided to their seating area, which was a bit larger than the other areas. Rose and Big Eaze seats were adorned in jewels of every color. The massive chairs were wrapped in gold fabric. Their seating was set inches above the main floor, which allowed them to look down to a party of two hundred guests. The guests would need to walk up about six steps to approach Rose. Of course, they didn't have to; Rose came down to meet the guests. Hugs and kisses were exchanged, and there was laughter throughout the ballroom. Everyone seemed to be having a good time; they were comfortable with their seating arrangements.

Some guests danced, some ate, some drank, and others just sat in amazement. Rose tried to greet everyone but it was impossible. She was pulled here and there. She danced with some guests and sat and talked with others.

DJ Spinn really pulled it off. He had all types of music playing; young and old could relate to his spinning. The night was magical; everyone had their moments with Rose. There were hugs and tears of joy; Rose was as happy as a kid.

People lined up to do the Electric Slide, Cha Cha Cha, and ballroom dancing. All types of group dancing could be seen on the ballroom floor; of course, Rose would join in. By the end of the night she would be exhausted. But she said, "I'm going to live it up and rest all day tomorrow."

Big Eaze walked over to DJ Spinn while he continued to spin the hottest hits. It seemed Big Eaze was asking for a specific song to be played. DJ Spinn nodded in agreement, and then Big Eaze walked back to Rose, he took her by the hand, and guided her to the ballroom floor. Big Eaze had chosen the song, "This One's for Me and You" by Johnny Gill featuring New Edition. It was the perfect song for them. Rose's favorite dance was the Two-Step, and she glided toward Big Eaze. He gently held Rose close to him and laid his hands on her waist while she swayed back and forth.

Ruby and Scarlet watched them dance, their faces filled with joy. Rose twirled and when the lights hit her gown, at that very moment, there it was, the sparkle of the rhinestones hit the lights and resonated a shimmering gold, dancing to the music of lights. Rose was right. She would look like a precious jewel dancing with her king. What a sight! Their faces said it all; they were mesmerized. Rose looked like a beautiful butterfly fluttering in the sky.

Everyone let the song play out before they were to go back to the ballroom floor. But before that moment, Big Eaze kneeled, reached into his tuxedo pocket, and pulled out a white box. He opens it and Ruby could see from where she was standing that ROCK, an engagement ring!

Big Eaze had just proposed to Rose on her fiftieth birthday. I guess you're never too old to find love. She blushed and said yes! Rose bowed to a crowd that stood up cheering, clapping, whistling, and tossing rose petals at their feet.

Chapter 20

Dancing Machine

AFTER THAT BEAUTIFUL SONG, the very next selection was "Happy People" by R. Kelly. Everyone was too joined in the dance. Most people kept up with that song; everyone was in sync with the movement. Each face had a big grin, bigger than a smiley face emoji. There were people looking at other people's feet (just to get the dance right). They stepped to the left and stepped to the right, spun around brought it down!

Spinn would not let anyone go back to their seats; the very next selection was "Champagne Life." He was such a great DJ; he knew what to play and when to play it.

The servers brought out trays of glasses filled with champagne, giving one to every guest who was age appropriate. DJ Spinn played "One Dance" by Drake. While walking toward the dance floor backward, he pointed to Ruby as if to say, "I need one dance." … lol oh ok I'm feeling the champagne effect Ruby thought,

I'll let him have this one dance, seeing as how this is a special occasion. But he will get an ear full later! Best believe, buddy, you're gonna get it!

The song lyrics said, "Time of our lives" and they sure were in the midst of having the time of their lives! They danced and danced and dance ... ain't no stopping us now we're on move When the song "24K Magic" played, woo they hit the floor with that song, popping their shoulders at "Twenty-four karat, twenty-four karat magic, what's that sound?" They were feeling it!

Rose started a Soul Train line when DJ Spinn played "I Feel Like Bustin' Loose." More and more joined in. So many dance songs played: "Can't Touch This," "I'm Coming Out," "Let's Get It Started," "Moves Like Jagger," "Worth It." He played one of Rose's favorite songs: "Somebody" by Natalie La Rose. Actually, he played many of Rose's favorite songs. The dance moves were hilarious, and the guests had a really good time!

I felt the music slowly slowing down due to his selection seem to be geared to an older crowd. He played "Slow Jams" by Quincy Jones.

I sure didn't think that people still slow dance but I guess wrong they were dancing!

Here's another one of Rose favorite song & by the look of it, it was everyone song. The guest still partner up & dance their heart out to "Lay with you" by El Debarge.

It's a sight to see when you see a bunch of couples doing the Swing dance (a great song) thought Ruby

Though we stood off from the crowd I continue to scan the ballroom There were people dancing, seated, eating, talking, and just mingling. The looks on the guest's faces were of pure pleasure. They seemed to be comfortable, relaxed, just having a fabulous evening out.

We stood there in awe of a place that seemed to be taken right out of a romance novel.

We wanted the setting to be set in a soft view, filled with elegance & class, which spoke of Rose & her life style.

They thought, *We did it! And did it well.* The divas were pleased, giving each other a high-five.

Chapter 21

Time for Cake

It was announced by the high-squealing annoying announcer (who hired him) that it was that time to sing the birthday song. Rose was guided to the middle of the floor. She stood next to a cake made to look like roses of every color of the rainbow. It was absolutely beautiful. Everyone in their splendor stood tall, ready to burst out that song. The announcer instructed everyone to begin singing at the count of three. He used his fingers for the countdown. All two hundred guests sang.

"HAPPY BIRTHDAY TO YOU
HAPPY BIRTHDAY TO YOU
HAPPY BIRTHDAY TO ROOSSEE
HAPPY BIRTHDAY TO YOUUUU!"

Everyone clapped and Rose thanked everyone. She said, "That was beautiful. Now please join me and have some of this cake. I can't eat it all."

The cake was guided back to a very long table and cut in pieces for each guest to enjoy. Soft music played in the background while the guests continued to mingle; laughter could be heard throughout the castle. The guests hurried to get a piece of the cake. One said, "I'm sure that the cake is as delicious as it looks."

While the guests were getting a piece of cake, the hosts and hostesses were to place thank-you notes on each table. The cards were emoji thank-you cards asking how they were feeling today. Ruby and Scarlet always tried to keep the events in a happy mood. The cards were to thank the guests for joining in this special occasion. It sure would be a surprise to see them all mailed back to Rose. With special written notes on them.

The castle lights came on and Rose stood to address the guests, thanking them all for sharing this special day with her. She thanked DJ Spinn for the awesome music selections. She added, "I'm very exhausted. Would you say the same?" pointing to the guests. Everyone said yes at the same time.

Letting DJ Spinn know that he did an awesome job!

Rose thanked the food preparers the hosts and hostesses. "You did such a great job tonight. Thank you for patience. Thank you for your outstanding diligence in staying professional in this large gathering!" She thanked the guests for the gifts of laughter and the gift of generosity. She said, "It was a joy to have you share this special day with me. Thank you!"

Rose turned to her daughters and, with both hands out, she bowed before them and blew kisses to them. She placed her hands on her heart and became very emotional. She thanked them for all they had done and all they had achieved and would keep achieving. She thanked them for the gift of motherhood, being allowed to mother them, saying it had been a joy.

Scarlet, Ruby, and Bubbles walked to her and surrounded her with love, hugs, and kisses. They received a big round of applause.

Chapter 22

A Perfect Ending

THE NIGHT WAS ENDING and DJ Spinn played, "That's What I Like" by Bruno Mars. People continued to dance while others picked up their belongings and headed out through the massive gold doors singing, "Lucky for you that's what I like!"

The music could be heard outdoors. DJ Spinn had speakers placed outside, neatly lined on the beautiful green manicured lawn. Under a full moon, the beautiful sets of lights that adorned the outside of the castle flickered as if they were candles flickering in the Hawaiian breeze.

Get this it ain't over, DJ Spinn played "Cake by the Ocean" by DNCE, a fitting song, seeing as how Rose's party was in a castle overlooking the ocean.

Laughing out loud we all stop looked at each other, and joined in dancing to this perfect ending set in a perfect setting. "CAKE BY THE OCEAN ooohh aaahhhhh ya ya ya ya ya… and again we sing "CAKE BY

THE OCEAN" oooohhh aaaahhhh ya ya ya ya ya…" Everyone, young and old, bellowed out "CAKE BY THE OCEAN…" The clean version, of course. Rose wouldn't have it any other way.

The End

About the Author

Carla M. Cuffee resides in the City of Champions, Pittsburgh, Pennsylvania. She has two adult children and one young grandchild. Her hobbies include reading, writing, and creating her view of art.

Acknowledgments

My two daughters, Kenya S. Garner and Shaterra M. Freelove; and granddaughter, SaNiya M. Matthews.

To my mother, Betty R. Banks; and father, Eugene Moss.

I believe they all took part in my creative mind-set.